for Jonathan with love—S.L.-J.
for Rachel—D.K.

Text copyright © 2009 by Sally Lloyd-Jones
Illustrations copyright © 2009 by Dan Krall

Published by Schwartz & Wade Books,
an imprint of Random House Children's Books, a division of Random House, Inc., New York.

Schwartz & Wade Books and colophon are trademarks of Random House, Inc.

Visit us on the Web! www.randomhouse.com/kids
Educators and librarians, for a variety of teaching tools, visit us at www.randomhouse.com/teachers

Library of Congress Cataloging-in-Publication Data
Lloyd-Jones, Sally.
Being a pig is nice : a child's-eye view of manners / Sally Lloyd-Jones ; illustrated by Dan Krall. — 1st ed.
p. cm.
Summary: Tired of being told to be polite and to not misbehave, a child considers
trading places with various animals and a monster.
ISBN 978-0-375-84187-3 (trade) — ISBN 978-0-375-94590-8 (Gibraltar lib. bdg.)
[1. Behavior—Fiction. 2. Etiquette—Fiction. 3. Animals—Fiction. 4. Humorous stories.] I. Krall, Dan, ill. II. Title.
PZ7.L77878Be 2009
[E]—dc22
2008006693

The text of this book is set in Magna Carta.
The illustrations are lovingly painted in Photoshop.
Book design by Rachael Cole

MANUFACTURED IN CHINA
10 9 8 7 6 5 4 3 2 1
First Edition

being a pig is nice

A CHILD'S-EYE VIEW OF MANNERS

written by Sally Lloyd-Jones   drawn by Dan Krall

schwartz & wade books · new york

When you're a kid it's not good
because your mom is always telling you,

But what if I were a PIG?

When you're a PIG
it's not polite to be clean.
It is Very Rude.
You have to get muddy
or you get in trouble.

But when you're a pig you smell
and that's not nice.

What if I were a SNAIL?

Walking fast isn't polite when you are a SNAIL.
It is Thoughtless and Inconsiderate.
You have to dawdle and crawl and trail behind
and not keep up with the others
or you get in trouble.

And when you're racing along,
your daddy will say,

But you are slimy when you're a snail
and that's not nice.

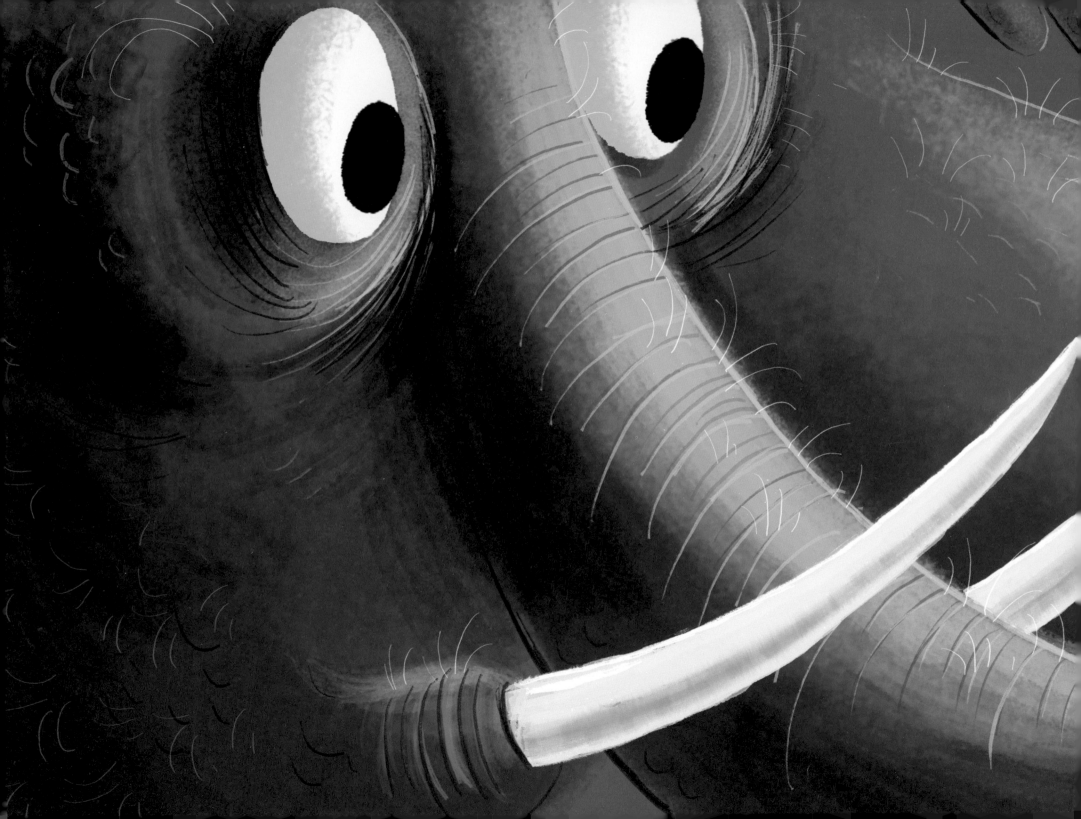

What if I were an ELEPHANT?

When you're an ELEPHANT
It is polite to splash.
Not splashing is Atrocious,
Disgraceful Conduct.

You have to squirt and splatter everyone
and be very naughty in your bath
or you get in trouble.
And if you don't, your daddy will shout,

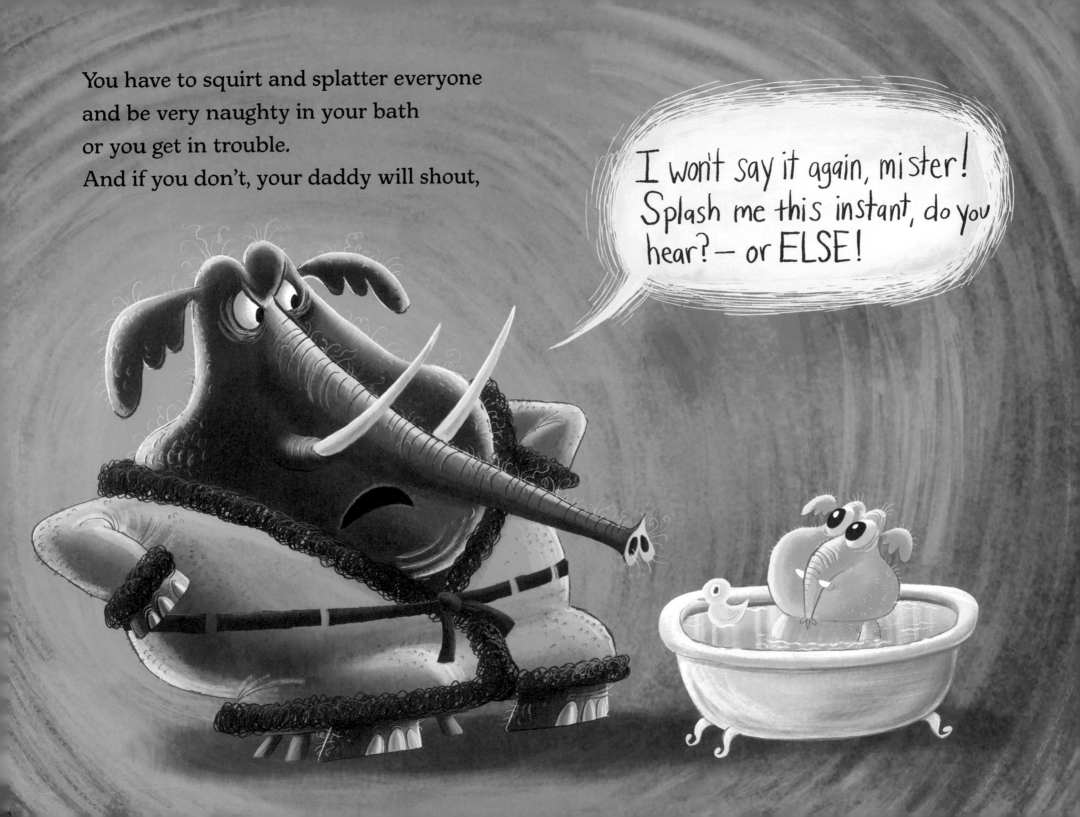

But flies and all their relations come to live on you when you're an elephant and that's not nice.

What if I were a MONKEY?

When you're a MONKEY
eating with a knife and fork isn't allowed.
It's Against The Rules.

You must always use your fingers
(that's what they're there for)
or you get in trouble.

But you have to eat grubs out of
everyone's ears when you're a monkey
and that's not nice.

Maybe I could be an OWL.

If you are an OWL
being quiet at night isn't being good.
It's Completely Inexcusable Behavior.

But you have to eat mice for breakfast
and then throw up their fur
and bones if you are an owl
and that's not nice.

I could always
be a MONSTER!

And you can do anything you want

(as long as it's Bad and Naughty and Awful and Monstrous).

And when you're perfectly terrible,
your monster mom will kiss
your monster cheek and say,

Oh, my own dear darling
dreadful disgusting horrible
rude little monster!

And whatever I do when I'm a monster,
I must not ever remember
and never bring with me
and always forget . . .

my MANNERS.
(Because it's only polite!)